Killer Feet

By Princess Kink

Killer Feet
Copyright © 2021 Princess Kink

Table of Contents

Chapter 1: Blazing Lust

Tatiana was getting ready to leave her motel room when the manager knocked on the door. A deafening thud could be heard followed by a high-pitched male scream. "Jesus Christ! What did you do to my door!" yelled the motel manager, peering into the darkness of the motel room. The curtains were closed, rendering the room almost completely dark. Tatiana opened the bathroom door and walked in with nothing but a towel around her torso and another wrapped around her wet hair. She'd just gotten out of the shower. The manager studied her body from head to toe.

"What seems to be the problem?" asked Tatiana, in an innocent and slightly erotic voice.

The motel manager stuttered as he pointed at the door hanging off its last hinge. "W-What is the problem? Isn't it obvious? Someone filed a complaint last night, saying that there was a loud noise like a door being kicked in. I didn't get around to checking it out until this morning. What happened?" he said, almost out of breath from his longwinded rant about the obvious. His hair was greasy and thinning above his temples. When he caught Tatiana looking at him, he seemed ashamed. Ashamed of his walrus-like body and hairy arms and neck.

"I don't have a lot of money…surely there's something else I could do for you," she said as she dropped the towel wrapped around her torso. The motel manager's jaw literally dropped at the sight of her gorgeous body. Her breasts, legs, curvy waist and freshly shaved pussy were enough to distract his attention away from the scars on her belly. He didn't care. This was the first time in a long time he'd seen a woman like this naked in person. Normally, he'd only be able to see women like this as they starred in a kinky porno. "So, what will it be? I won't have sex with you, and I won't blow you. There must be something else you like. Another body part or fantasy perhaps that you've been too embarrassed to act on thus far?" Tatiana pointed her toes down and moved her left flexed foot up and down her right calf. She then caressed herself with her hands and slapped her own ass cheeks.

"I-I-I…" stuttered the motel manager, pulling a handkerchief out of his pocket and soaking up the sweat from his forehead with it.

"Ass? Foot? Leg? Tits? Hands? All of them can give you a job," said Tatiana, adding in a seductive moan for good measure. Normally, she would've loved to kill this pathetic slob of a man and be done with it. But she didn't want to draw any attention to herself. She moved in closer when he failed to answer her. "Let's find out together." She grabbed the fat manager's fat hands and placed them on her naked breasts. Her nipples had hardened with the cool air coming from the air conditioner. He let out an ugly moan, bordering on a choke. For him, it was as if the porn he normally watched had come to life, fulfilling his desires one by one.

She pulled his hands lower towards her hips, making sure to avoid the scars on her belly. She slapped her ass cheeks with his hands. "Grab them…mean it," she said in a stern tone. He instantly obeyed her command and grabbed her cheeks as hard as he could, leaving handprints on her delicate skin. "Get on your knees!" she yelled. The motel manager didn't know why he was obeying her commands when it was her who owed him a favor, but something deep down inside him went along with it. Something that wanted to serve his queen, no matter what she told him to do. Tatiana could've ordered him to jump off a cliff and if he were mesmerized enough in the moment, he actually would have done so. "You're now mine, do you understand?" she hissed at him, her beautiful curves blocking out the rest of the room, pinpointing his focus on the body of his newfound mistress.

"Yes mistress," he answered.

"Open your mouth, slave!" He opened his mouth as wide as it could possibly go. Tatiana spat into the back of his throat. He savored her sweet spit before swallowing it. "Did I tell you to close your mouth? Keep it open!" she yelled at him, delivering a swift kick to his balls that left him groaning on the floor. "Don't be such a baby! That was nothing!" The motel manager scrambled back up to his knees. "Show me," said Tatiana, pointing at his pants. He quickly pulled his pants off and slid his underwear off as well, revealing a surprisingly juicy cock with low hanging, hairy balls that looked as though they hadn't been properly drained of their white seed in ages.

Tatiana slapped her bare foot against his wide ballsack once again, sending the motel manager groaning to the floor for a second time. "I-I can't take it…it hurts too much!" he grunted into the carpet. He'd watched ballbusting porn many times and enjoyed the thought of being powerless and vulnerable against a woman, but being on the receiving end of it for the first time in his life was something different entirely.

"You'll get used to it. I need to desensitize you first, which can only be achieved through more kicks, slaps, and punched to those beautiful balls of yours." Tatiana placed her foot on the motel manager's forehead and moved her sole down to his nose and lips. "Stick your tongue out." He licked between each of her toes and cleaned the entirety of the bottom of her foot. He then proceeded to suck on her toes, finishing her foot off by deepthroating as much of her foot as he could before gagging. He then turned his attention to the other foot, giving it the exact same treatment.

Tatiana then placed her spit covered foot on his forehead again and pushed him down to the floor so that he was lying flat on his back. She positioned herself over his head while facing his now erect cock. It was a good size, and even though he was a slob, she kind of wanted to taste it. She sat on his face, making sure that he got a good taste of her pink asshole. With her feet, she gave him a slow footjob, pulling and pushing his foreskin up and down. The motel manager let out a muffled moan into the dark tunnel of her tight ass. The sensual footjob grew more intense as Tatiana upped the speed.

The fat slob, buried deep within her poop shoot, thrusted his hips up and down as the cum started to pump out of his cock in thick, creamy strings. Tatiana liked the feeling of hot cum on her feet and between her toes, like nature's slippery lotion. The motel manager grabbed her hips and tried to push her off his face. He couldn't breathe and was on the verge of losing consciousness.

Tatiana couldn't help herself. She hated this useless man, willing to settle for sex instead of hearing out her side of the story as to how the door was broken in the first place. She let go and turned around, quickly positioning one of her legs behind his neck. Before he could catch his breath, she pulled his mouth into her pussy and locked her other leg behind the leg wrapped around the back of his neck. She moaned as the motel manager writhed around, trying to escape her triangle

—

choke, her pussy juices dripping down his chin and all over the carpet as if a snail had been squeezed dry of all her mucus. She came right as he died, his entire head swollen into a purple mess. She had to grind out the last part of her orgasm on the dead man's lips and quivered with sensitivity and sweat. So much for not drawing any attention to herself. She'd just killed the motel manager and left a healthy amount of DNA everywhere.

She rolled off his dead corpse and lay down next to him, panting. She looked into his dead eyes and smiled. "Dead over a stupid door," she whispered in between breaths. She then wedged the chair in the corner of the room against the front door in case it decided to completely give out. She couldn't afford to be caught stupidly. Tatiana quickly showered and cleaned the carpet as well as the motel manager's body the best she could, before gathering her belongings and pulling the matchbox from her coat pocket. She lit all the matches and threw them on the carpet before calmly exiting the room, ensuring that the door didn't release from its last hinge.

It took the fire department about half an hour to receive the call and show up. By then, the entire room had been brought down to a black crisp. The motel manager's body looked like a Thanksgiving fried turkey accident. There wasn't much the police could've gathered from his soot covered bones.

Chapter 2: High Heel

Officer John Donovan was still out in the city with Violet wrapped around his body like a coiled tropical viper. They'd decided to stay overnight in a hotel together which John naturally paid for. They'd had sex two more times in the late hours of the night, sucking, fondling, sniffing, and licking everything that their little hearts desired. John's phone rang, startling the two lovers out of their head splitting hangover. Violet had ended up joining John in his drinking frenzy.

"Hello?" John groaned into the phone, his eyes still closed.

"Where are you? I've been ringing you for hours!" said Nathan.

"I-I didn't go home last night. I'm still in the city. What's up?" replied John, pushing Violet's shiny leg off of his thigh. His cock was still out and slightly stuck to the bedsheets due to the drying of bodily fluids.

"We may have another lead. Motel in El Cerrito burned down earlier this morning. The room where the fire started was being paid for by a young woman. She had used the name Larissa Johnson, a fake name that led us to a dead end. Get this, her next-door neighbor said that he'd briefly seen her the night that she'd checked in. Young, beautiful woman with long brown hair, wearing a purple dress. She had bare legs and wore high heels. He said that the purple dress had a vintage middle school uniform sort of look to it. Sound familiar?"

John instantly sat up. His headache had almost completely disappeared. "No way it's our girl. She can't be that stupid."

"We found the body of the motel manager burned to shit. Maybe he walked in on her and saw something that he wasn't supposed to, and she had no choice but to kill him and set fire to her room to dispose of the evidence and DNA. I texted you the address." John hung up on Nathan and pulled himself up to his feet with a groan.

"Everything okay?" asked Violet, looking up at John from her pillow.

"Everything is fine. Something came up, I need to leave immediately. I'll pay for another day. You can sleep in and leave whenever you want to," replied John without turning around to look at her. He knew that if he did, he'd get sucked back into the lust of her perfect body and face. Violet poked John in his lower back with her flexed big toe. She then wrapped her foot around his shoulder and twirled him around. Before he could make another excuse, she placed both her feet behind his neck and slowly pulled him in towards her shaved, pink pussy. He ate it for breakfast, tasting not just her but the remnants of himself surviving within the droplets of those heavenly pussy juices. She came almost instantly, forcing John to redirect his attention away from her sensitive clit. He shoved his entire tongue into her pussy instead, tasting those salty sweet walls. He flexed his tongue, working her up to her second orgasm.

"I want you inside me. I want him inside me," she moaned as she grabbed his hand, placing his index finger into her mouth to suck on. She pulled him up towards her chest and grabbed his cock and balls. She moved down, replacing John's index finger with his hardening cock. She sucked it profusely as if she were participating in a blowjob contest. John was surprised that his cock was still able to get hard after the previous night's multiple sessions. When he was hard enough, she guided him into her pussy with her hand. John thrusted five times before her pussy tightened around his throbbing cock. Violet dug her fingernails into his back and opened her mouth wide. She made no sound as she flexed every muscle in her body, cumming yet again.

She pushed John out of her pussy and into her mouth, giving him one of the best blowjobs he'd ever received. The only thing that made it not the best was the fact that his cockhead was very desensitized due to the number of times he'd cum in one night. He came loudly inside her cheek. It was a very watery load that Violet was able to swallow with ease. She squeezed out every last drop from the base of his penis, moving her hand up slowly towards the sensitive tip.

John gave her a kiss on the cheek and hurried out of the hotel room. As promised, he extended his stay by another day, paying an extra fee for the last-minute notice. He didn't care. Money meant nothing to John. Only justice and bodily pleasures.

"Late night again?" asked Nathan, looking at John's unkempt hair and pale face. Any energy and nutrients he might've had were surely being digested in Violet's stomach.

"What do we got?" said John, ignoring Nathan's own addiction for his partner's personal life.

"Other than what I already told you on the phone, nothing. Nothing new. No DNA. No knife or other clues that survived the fire. She set fire to the room in a very strategic way, making sure that the flames spread to all corners of her motel room. Nothing survived, not even the teeth of the motel manager, disallowing us from matching any of his dental records. The only reason that we know it's him is because he's the only one who is currently missing. His name was Abraham Dias."

"What about security footage? Any cameras?" asked John, looking up at the remaining corners of the black and soot covered building.

"The tapes are missing. She knew what she was doing. She took them before she left the premises." John sighed. Another lost opportunity with zero real clues.

"There must be something! A traffic camera or something that captured a license plate or a clear picture of her," said John, checking the nearby traffic lights and intersection. There was indeed a camera that might've captured something.

"Already on that," said Nathan. "So far, nothing. She didn't drive here. We found some bushes behind the building with snapped twigs and branches. She left through the back on foot, and before you ask, no there were no shoe or footprints." John slapped his knee and looked at Nathan with annoyed eyes.

"There must be something…Something that we're missing. A hair. Dead skin cells on the broken twigs and branches. Something! Are there any other traffic cameras out back?"

"No. DNA wouldn't do us any good either. She's unregistered in our records, an illegal. Maybe she's here for a limited time and her orders were to kill Andrew Lewis. This motel manager seems like something unplanned. Normally, assassins will not get paid if the body of the victim cannot be identified, which in the case of the motel manager definitely holds true. You'd have more luck identifying a mummy!"

A mummy thought John. They needed something preserved, something riddled with clues in plain sight. The Russian Mafia instantly came to mind. Someone within their organization had to know who this mystery woman was. Nathan seemed to read his mind. "John…no. You cannot go after them. They'll kill you, do you understand me!"

John wasn't listening anymore. He hurried back to his car and keyed the engine. Then, he caught a glimpse of the damnedest thing. A homeless man lay in the alleyway across the street from the parking lot. Something was off about him. He was still, too still…almost as if he were a mummy waiting to be discovered. Nathan knocked on John's window and tried to open the door. "C'mon man, you gotta stop being so reckless!"

John stepped out of the car without acknowledging his partner and crossed the street. He was right. The moment he stepped into the alleyway of miscreants, he noticed that the homeless man's sleeping bag was soaked in blood. He'd been stabbed in the heart, the exact same wound that'd shown Mr. Lewis his end. That wasn't the most interesting clue, however. John's heart skipped a beat when he saw what was lying next to the wall, stuffed away like a piece of fresh trash: a black high heel. John approached it as if it were the Holy Grail. He gestured Nathan and the rest of the team to come over and pointed at the heel with an ear-to-ear grin.

"Bag it immediately and let me know what the results are as soon as they come in. Run everything, every single test that you can!" John watched as they bagged the high heel and carried it off to the lab. "I told you that there had to be something."

"Yea, you did. Don't gloat. Something tells me that those tests aren't gonna tell us shit. She's a ghost…our mystery woman," said Nathan, itching his balding head. Both detectives suddenly felt embarrassed and guilty that they'd paid no attention to the dead man lying on the cold and dirty stone of the alleyway before their feet. His face looked peaceful, as if death had been a sweet relief. He probably saw her leaving or startled her, and the mystery woman didn't want any witnesses. John imagined what he must've last seen: a gorgeous young woman, hurrying along into an alleyway that she shouldn't have, getting caught up in an altercation that she shouldn't have. How had the heel come off?

Chapter 3: Trust Me

Tatiana waited anxiously for her handler. She normally didn't call for help, but this was an emergency. She'd just killed someone on the streets in cold blood. "Don't worry," said the distorted voice on the other end of the line. She called her emergency number via a payphone in San Francisco. She'd called a cab immediately after her incident with the homeless man in the alley.

She remembered the way his voice had startled her as she was making her getaway. "Where are you off to sweetheart?" he'd said from the shadows of the dark alleyway. Tatiana had ignored him, but the drunk fool had groped her, swiping at her legs with his dirt covered arms and hands. He'd caught her right heel, ripping it off of her foot. With his other hand, he'd latched onto her ankle, rubbing and caressing her bare leg. The homeless man hadn't had a decent meal in years, but having her shiny, sexy leg in his hand had instantly hardened his cock. He'd taken it out and that's when Tatiana had lost it. She'd kicked him in the face with her other heel, but the man wouldn't let go. He was so horny that not even pain thwarted his attacks. Without even knowing it, Tatiana had slipped her knife into his heart, killing him instantly.

Tatiana finally arrived at the address that her handler had given to her over the phone. She was never allowed to write down addresses such as these, or any information that her handler passed onto her in confidence. Sinful Eden she whispered to herself, looking up at the neon sign. A man was waiting for her at the back entrance and gestured for her to approach. He looked at her dirty bare feet. Her soles were almost black from the dirt and uncleanliness clung to her skin like a filthy disease. She'd stuffed her remaining heel into the small purse she carried around. "It's a long story," she said as she walked past him.

Inside Sinful Eden, the bass from the club music was pounding through the walls. Some of the girls walked by Tatiana, giving her a weird look. All the women working at the club were like one big family. Any outsiders were instantly scrutinized, especially if there was something off about them, like dirty bare feet in a city like San Francisco.

The club owner's wife, whom the ladies called Mother, walked in to vet this new girl. She was about to begin her usual routine of putting Tatiana through a few different tests, which included seeing if her husband's cock got hard as the new girl danced. Her husband, club owner Armand Petrosian, looked nervous around this new arrival. "Do not test her," he said to his wife. "Instead, teach her a few things about dancing and how business works around here so that she'll fit in right away."

Mrs. Maddie Petrosian looked her husband in the eyes, taken aback by this unusual request. "Who is she? Can she even dance? Have you forgotten that it is my job to vet out any new girls who want to join our family?"

"Be quiet and do as I say. Don't ask any questions and for the love of God, do not piss her off. It's been arranged. She'll be staying with us for a while. Just teach her how things work…please." Armand grabbed his wife's hands with a slight look of fear in his eyes. She'd never seen him like this before. She looked at Tatiana and then at her dirty bare feet. The strange new girl's eyes were as cold as the grave.

"Fine," she whispered to her husband without breaking her gaze. "First, she'll need to wash up. Sweetie, what's your shoe size?" she asked in a motherly voice. It was this voice that had earned her the nickname, Mother.

"Seven," replied Tatiana, fishing her remaining heel out of her purse.

"Have you ever walked in eight-inch stripper heels before?"

Tatiana shook her head and then looked at the clock on the wall. She was tired and hungry and in much need of washing up. "Follow me," said Maddie, leading Tatiana into the back and away from the rest of the girls' curious eyes. "You can wash up here. I'll go and get you some heels and an outfit so you can start dancing tonight." Tatiana stripped down in front of Maddie, who was instantly drawn to the scars on her belly and hip.

"Get me an outfit that's not too revealing," said Tatiana, turning on the showerhead in the girls' dressing room. Right before she stepped into the shower, she turned around and looked at Maddie. "I'm going to leave my purse and belongings on the counter here. If you or anyone touches or looks through my stuff, there'll be hell to pay!" Maddie would normally have the upper hand in her conversations with her girls, but there was no denying that Tatiana's threatening presence made her the alpha in this particular situation.

"What did you do!" screamed Maddie at her husband in their soundproof office in the very back of the club.

"Nothing! She'll be out of here before you know it," replied Armand, covering the side of his face in case his wife decided to slap him.

"She's barking orders and threatening me! I don't like her! Why does she need to be a dancer? If we're hiding her or whatever this is, why not just have her hang out in this room?"

"Because I'm terrified, okay!" yelled Armand, slamming his big hairy fist onto the desk. "She's involved with the Russians…a killer…someone worth hiding for a great sum of money. I don't want her snooping around in here or anywhere near me for that matter! What if she decides to kill me or you?" Maddie's face went pale, and her pupils doubled in size.

"You brought a killer into our home? What the fuck is wrong with you! Why are you getting involved with the Russians again! You promised me that you'd set some clear boundaries with those nutjobs!"

"Shh!" hissed Armand, jumping up to his feet and placing his palm over Maddie's mouth. "You never know who might be listening…"

"The room is soundproof you dingbat!" growled Maddie, ripping his hand off her face.

"Look…" said Armand, gently grabbing his wife's palms. "You trust me, right? This is temporary. She just needs a place to lie low until things clear up a bit. She'll just be another one of the girls. She isn't here for the money, so she doesn't have to dance on stage or anything. She'll just blend in with the rest of the girls, like white noise in the background. Then, the Russians will owe me one, and it is good to not piss off those who'll protect you. How do you think we survived all these years? The Russians have always protected our club and watched our back since the beginning. It'll be fine…trust me." Maddie wanted to trust her husband as she once did, but something about this felt wrong. Armand had gotten too greedy over the years and taken more risks than she was comfortable with, almost getting them both killed twice.

—

"Whatever you say, my love. If one thing goes wrong or if she spooks or threatens me again, she's out on the streets!" said Maddie right before she opened the door and slammed it behind her, not allowing any time for Armand to respond.

It turned out that Tatiana didn't have any trouble whatsoever with moving her body in the slithering and curvy ways that make men drool. She was a trained assassin after all and knowing these sorts of tactics of lust was definitely a must. Maddie didn't have to give her any pointers, but her gaze kept getting drawn to Tatiana's belly. No matter how many outfits she had the mystery girl try on, none of them fully covered up the scars on her belly. Maddie's thoughts turned to makeup. Maybe with just enough makeup, she could cover them up. Especially with the way the club lights always masked the imperfections of the skin.

"Why do I need to dance?" said Tatiana, climbing down from the pole. She was extremely talented and agile with the pole, grinding and pressing her body against it with more passion than any of the other girls.

"Because you need to put in work around here just like everyone else," lied Maddie, spewing out her fake words with disgust. She wholeheartedly agreed with Tatiana. Why did she have to dance? If she was caught up in some illegal shit, wouldn't it be more beneficial to have her hide in the back?

—

"You're lying," said Tatiana, peering into Maddie's eyes, causing the Mother to melt away inside herself like plastic melting over an open fire. "You're scared of me. You don't trust me. You don't want me roaming in the backrooms with the quiet and shadows on my side. You want me out in the open, exposed on the dancefloor…so that if anything goes wrong, you'll have time to make your escape."

Maddie opened her mouth, but nothing came out. Only a slight croak. "Don't worry. I'm not angry. I have my own orders," said Tatiana with a cruel smile.

Evening rolled through like a foreboding curse. All the girls got ready in the changing rooms, putting makeup on and helping each other with their newly revealing outfits. Tatiana sat in the corner, holding the two outfits that Maddie had issued her with, along with the clear, plastic stripper heels. The other girls whispered to each other and stared at her like the new arrival of a classroom. "Do you need some help?" asked one of the more senior girls by the name of Lauren, though her stage name was Violet.

Tatiana looked up at her and nodded. "I don't know which one to wear." Violet gestured for Tatiana to stand up, and all the girls gasped the moment she did. They all saw her scars and shook their heads with anger and pity. A lot of the girls had come from broken families, beaten, exiled, and raped. Seeing scars like that reminded them of their origins, and for others, Tatiana's disfigurement was a shocking awakening to reality. It reminded them of how easily their profession could be taken away from them. One cut, one horrible altercation, one maiming and it would all be over.

The rest of the girls huddled around Tatiana, accepting this veteran of abuse as one of their own. They all looked at the two outfits and spoke amongst themselves about which one would cover her up the best. One was a black lace bodysuit, which also doubled as a short dress at the same time, that was a tad bit see-through around the belly. The chest area had an old 80s looking furry patch. The other outfit looked like a white and very see-through nightgown with a fishnet waistband at the bottom designed to hug a woman's plump buttocks with sexual grill marks.

"Go with the black," said Violet, looking down at Tatiana's bare feet. Her toenails had lost a lot of their nail polish from running barefoot through the streets and bushes. Violet clicked her tongue at one of the girls, telling her to bring her a bottle of nail polish. The ladies at this particular club really took care of one another, which wasn't always the case at strip clubs. In record time, they had helped Tatiana with her new outfit, her makeup, and given her a quick pedicure. She waited there with her fingers between her toes, waiting for them to dry, while Violet found her some new heels.

"Here" she said, handing Tatiana her new pair of heels which Violet had been kind enough to provide. They were black heels with black and silver straps, which were much more comfortable to walk in than the eight-inch stripper heels that Maddie had originally proposed. The dayshift girls trickled in and were slowly swapped out with the nightshift staff. Tatiana waited to go last and made her way to the second floor. She acted shy but lurked in the darkness with a plan. "Come, why don't you join me? We can tag team the first few customers. I'll show you the ropes," said Violet, taking Tatiana by the hand. "What's your stage name? You gotta have a stage name."

Tatiana thought for a minute, before replying with "Candy," in honor of the sex worker whom she'd almost fallen in love with.

They both sat down and grinded against their first customer; a fat old man by the name of Mark, who always drooled when any of the girls passed him by. "He's an ass man," whispered Violet in Tatiana's ear. "What do you think hun? Is tonight the night?" Violet moaned and ran her fingers across Tatiana's back and ass, making sure to give her ass cheeks a loud smack.

Mark fished his wallet out of his pocket and opened it with an annoying grin, as if this act alone were the grand prize from the Pope himself. "You know what, it just might be sweetheart," he said with a heavy breath. Tatiana shuddered inside herself but didn't show it. She was a professional after all, just not in the profession that everyone around her assumed she was. Violet nudged Tatiana to follow her and the two ladies escorted the fat man up the stairs, causing him to breathe even louder. Once they were in the room, Violet started the show by grabbing her ankles and letting her violet hair dangle down like a waterfall from Heaven. She twerked and jiggled her ass, which in turn awakened Mark's cock, causing it to slither up his thigh and into his pocket.

Tatiana sprang into action. She grinded her ass against the bulge in the fat man's pants. Mark moaned and pretty soon, Tatiana could feel his sticky wetness on her ass cheeks. The precum oozing out of his penis was enough to collect by the glass. Mark looked up at her as if she were some sort of exotic beast. "I've never seen you here before," he said in between moans and increasingly heavy breathing. Violet looked worried. She didn't want the fat man to have a heart attack.

Mark unzipped his pants and pulled out a really thick cock. It was a great size with a luscious swollen head that was spewing precum this way and that. Violet slid her panties to the side so that Mark could get a good look at her pink asshole. He moved his face forward, until his nose almost touched her asshole. He sniffed loudly as his eyes rolled into the back of his head. He really was an ass man. Violet unclenched her asshole, allowing for more of the fragrance to seep up Mark's nose. The fat man had started to jack off profusely.

Every part of him jiggled as he hurriedly squeezed one off.

He then grabbed Tatiana by the waist with his free hand. Tatiana didn't like this, and it caught her by surprise. Before she knew what she was doing, Tatiana had kicked Mark in the throat with her heel. The fat man choked and coughed as he took a nosedive to the floor, clutching his throat with both hands, his cock still out and rubbing against everything that came in its way. "What did you do!" screamed Violet, dropping to her knees to help the distressed customer. "Don't just stand there, get some help!" she screamed, looking at Tatiana with enraged fire in her eyes.

Tatiana walked over and assessed Mark's throat. It had a deep purple bruise forming at the base of it. "He'll live," she said in a cold monotone. She then slipped off her heel and stepped on his now semi-erect cock. The precum got stuck to her toes and soles in long gooey strings. She then sat down on top of Mark and slid her panties to the side, cupping her hand gently around his cock and balls. "You don't mind, do you sweetheart?" she said to him, while moaning seductively. Mark had forgotten about the kick to his throat and couldn't believe what was happening. She was sliding his thick shaft up and down against her asshole, while using her ass cheeks as a guiding corridor for his cock. His balls hit her wet pussy, making them glisten with pussy juices.

Mark opened his mouth and started to pant like a dog. Tatiana could feel the wet cum shooting all over her arm and back, as it pattered onto the carpet like heavy rain. She held Mark's foreskin down, so that his sensitive cockhead remained exposed. With her other hand, she gave his juicy balls a squeeze to make sure that every last drop had truly been milked out.

After Tatiana pulled herself up to her feet, Violet instantly pulled her to the side. "You've got cum all over your arm and back!" she hissed at her. Violet got a couple of napkins and started wiping away the evidence the best she could, before the cum dried and stained her black dress. "We're not supposed to get physical with our customers. They'll throw you out if they see these cum stains all over you! This is a gentleman's club, not some sleazy whorehouse!"

"Thank you Violet and friend," said Mark, placing down a few clumped-up bills as their tip, before hurrying out of the room.

"Relax, no one is going to get into any trouble," replied Tatiana as she picked up the clumped-up bills and handed them over to Violet.

"You don't want your cut?" she asked with a raised eyebrow.

"No. That's for you. I'm sorry for causing a scene. I just don't like it when strangers grab me from behind…"

———

"Honey, you're in the wrong profession then. That's all they do to us strippers," said Violet with a giggle. "You're not ever gonna kick me like that, right?"

Tatiana smiled at her. "No, unless you try to grab me from behind. I call it the horse kick."

Violet laughed. They continued to make their rounds together, until someone familiar showed up, already intoxicated with plenty of whiskey. "John, I want you to meet Candy! She's new here but has already proven herself to be a good wingwoman with the gentlemen," said Violet, giving John a kiss on the cheek.

"Nice to meet you," said John, clearly intoxicated. He held out his hand. Tatiana took it with a smile. "What makes her the perfect wingwoman?" asked John, slightly slurring his words.

"Well, she's not the perfect wingwoman, at least not in the traditional sense. She knows how to fight and doesn't take shit from intoxicated customers…such as yourself," said Violet, giving John a playful slap on the cheek. John instantly looked a bit more sober. He looked Tatiana in the eyes, trying to decipher the true woman hidden behind the mask.

"Wanna buy us a drink?" she asked, trying to change the subject and break the awkward silence.

"Yes. Yes…let's get a round. I'll meet you ladies at the usual table," said John as he headed over to the bar. Something cold lived in the new girl's eyes. Something that seemed familiar yet so foreign at the same time.

Chapter 4: Glistening Death

John brought the drinks out to his regular table in the corner. Tatiana and Violet sat there like two vixens, ready to seduce the intoxicated cop out of his money. "So…Candy…When was your first day? I haven't seen you around before," said John, handing Tatiana her kamikaze before placing the other one in front of Violet.

"Tonight is my first night," she replied with a nervous chuckle and pronounced monotone.

"You shoulda seen her!" said Violet, drinking half of her kamikaze in one gulp. "You see that guy over there?" she said, pointing at Mark who had already moved onto his next girl and was enjoying a lap dance. "She kicked his ass! He grabbed her and she did some kind of karate kick or something…what did you call it again?"

"The horse kick," replied Tatiana, a bit uncomfortable that this information was being shared so openly with this man whom she barely knew.

"Really?" said John, looking Tatiana up and down. His gaze found her feet and he was lost in a trance. She had very pretty feet. The DJ got on the mic and called for Violet to go to the main stage.

"Can you pay for me to get the night off again sweetheart?" asked Violet, sitting on John's lap and gently brushing her hand over his soft cock, trying to wake up the monster. John wasn't interested at all, however. He was strictly focused on Tatiana as if a sixth sense had been triggered, and the alarm was blaring loud and clear in the back of his mind, quickly clawing its way to the front.

"Not tonight. If I keep paying like that, I'll be broke by the end of the week! Besides, I want to spend a bit of time with your new friend over here," said John without even looking at Violet. Violet gave Tatiana, then John an annoyed look. Perhaps befriending this new stranger was a bad idea. John seemed completely starstruck by her. Violet left without a word, clattering her heels loudly across the floor.

John looked down at Tatiana's feet again. "No stripper heels?" he asked, letting out a cold grunt as he ingested a huge gulp of whiskey. He was right. Her getup and especially her heels, made her stick out like a sore thumb. She looked more like one of the waitresses prancing around, collecting orders from drunk and rowdy customers, than a stripper.

Tatiana shook her head and took a small and polite sip from her drink. "So, where were you before this? A stripper at another club?" asked John. Tatiana started to feel very uncomfortable but didn't show it one bit on her face or through her body language.

"It's an embarrassing story and something that I'm trying to forget. Let's just say that this opportunity as a stripper is an upgrade from my previous life," she said in a very convincing way, even making sure to add a benign lip quiver at the very end of her performance. This would've been enough to deter most people from continuing this line of questioning, but not John. Once he had his mind set on something, he always followed through to the end, no matter what the cost or how socially awkward it got.

"Enlighten me. I really want to hear your story, so much so that I'll pay you for your time." He took out a bundle of bills and placed eighty dollars on the table. "Please…tell me." Tatiana took the money, even though she didn't want it. But to play the role of a desperate girl off the streets who upgraded herself by becoming a stripper, she needed to seem money hungry.

"I was on the streets, moving from pimp to pimp…beaten and reduced to almost nothing. I couldn't tell you how long I was wandering the streets like that, since I wasn't entirely sober. But what I can tell you, is that I'll never go back to that kind of life…not in a million years!" Tatiana gulped down her drink with pronounced anger, surfacing it perfectly as part of her role, and looked at John for another round. John, being the alcoholic gentleman that he was, instantly got up and got her another drink.

———

"Is that how you learned to do the 'horse kick' as you call it?" asked John as he returned with another kamikaze and a neat whiskey.

"Yes. When fending for yourself on the streets, you need to learn a few moves. Kicks are particularly effective, especially when aimed at the groin or other sensitive areas," said Tatiana with a dominatrix's grin. John laughed at her joke, but something still felt wrong and twisted inside his gut. "Look, she's finally on stage," said Tatiana, desperately trying to change the conversation. John turned around to see Violet climbing the poll, her perfect ass jiggling ever so slightly. She then grabbed the top of the poll with her thighs and hung upside down like a bat. With her gorgeous, curvy legs, she started to do the bicycle in midair! Sometimes, John as well as the rest of the intoxicated customers forgot how much talent and strength it takes to do the things that strippers do so naturally. Her violet hair hung straight down, causing the club lights to cascade off of it. John felt his cock beginning to wake up from its slumber.

"I'm gonna go sweetie. I got to make my rounds," said Tatiana, having barely touched her drink.

"Wait!" protested John. "I paid good money for your company. Stay…finish you drink. This place is always packed, and I'll pay you even more for your time. I'll make it worthwhile, I promise." John didn't like how desperate he'd just sounded saying that to a stripper whom he'd never met before until tonight. Tatiana wanted to refuse this, but she knew that she couldn't. John was close with Violet and she needed to fly under Violet's radar as well as everyone else's.

"Fine, but not too long, okay baby?" she said, taking her seat across from him again. They both watched Violet in silence for a bit, slowly sipping their drinks. Then, John randomly turned around to face Tatiana and stood up. "Let's go to a private room. I'll even put in a fat tip for you…and not the kind that you're thinking of," he slyly added in, making him sound even more douchey and pathetic.

"I—I"

"C'mon, it'll be fun!" he quickly added in, cutting her off. He took Tatiana by the hand and led her to one of the private rooms. The bouncers gave them both a look as John quickly shut the door behind him. He sat down on his regular leather couch and placed a large stack of money on top of his bulge. "I've been dying to see what you look like without that horrible imitation fur mini dress or whatever it is, that you have on."

Tatiana chuckled nervously and thought about making a run for it. Maybe she could convince the bouncers to throw him out. Instead, she walked over to him, making sure to exaggerate the sway of her hips, and got down on her knees right in front him. With her hands, she gently pulled his legs apart and took the stack of bills off his bulge with her mouth. She placed them on the floor and with her index finger and her thumb, she ever so gently unzipped John's pants and released his cock. It sprung up like an eager coiled snake, ready to trap its prey. Tatiana smiled and offered his hard cock a few strokes before pulling herself up to her feet. This kind of teasing always got the boys hot and sweaty.

She then did the best she could, trying to copy some of the dances that she'd seen Violet do in the previous private room as well as some of the other strippers on stage. Tatiana wasn't the best dancer, but she knew enough moves to get by convincingly. Besides, turning a man on who has his cock out and dripping isn't the hardest thing in the world. When she got ready to grind against his throbbing cockhead, John gently grabbed her wrist. "I wanna see you naked," he whispered. "I want to see your curvy female body in all of its glory." Tatiana looked back worried.

"It's not a pretty sight," she told him, blushing a bit.

"I'm sure it is beautiful," he quickly replied, as his hand moved from her wrist towards the bottom of her mini dress. He pulled up the hem of her dress and stopped the moment he saw her belly. He then continued, eyeing the many scars that made the uneasy feeling in his own belly even more prominent. He knew how to read scars from a long career. He knew what knife cuts and gunshot wounds looked and felt like. "You've been shot before…multiple times," he said, looking Tatiana in the eye. The hardness of his cock had started to dwindle away as his focus as an officer returned. "Did that happen on the streets as well? Is it normal to get stabbed and shot as a lady of the streets and survive through what looks like self-inflicted stitches? What's your name? Your real name!" he said, grabbing her wrist again. Tatiana tried to pull away, but his grip only grew tighter.

Right then, the door to the private room opened. Tatiana immediately played the role of the victim as she fell to her knees and begged for John to let go. She was even able to produce a couple of tears that streamed down her cheeks and onto the carpet below. "John! What are you doing!" screamed Violet, grabbing his hand. She did her best to pry his fingers off Tatiana's wrist, but it was no use. His grip had coiled around his victim like the constrictions of a python. He then went for Tatiana's feet.

"Let me smell them!" he screamed like a madman.

"Help!" yelled Violet. "Help us!"

Tatiana pulled her feet away with one sweep and kicked John onto his back. The off-duty cop got back up to his feet, ready for a fight. He didn't receive the fight that he was looking for, however. Two bouncers walked in and restrained the drunk cop. "What are you doing? Get off of me! It's her! It's HER!" yelled John, as he was dragged away through the back entrance this time. He found himself on his ass out by the trashcans as the club's backdoor was slammed shut and locked.

"Fuck you!" he yelled, picking up a stone and throwing it as hard as he could against the metal door. John stumbled down the alleyway out back where he was met by three shadowy figures. He couldn't quite make out their faces as they spoke Russian amongst themselves. "W-What do you w-want," he slurred as his last drink of whiskey finally caught up to him. They replied with three metal pipes. John found himself on the ground again, drenched in his own blood as the pipes slammed and smashed into his skull, arms, legs, and torso. He screamed for help but was instantly muffled by a swift strike to the face, cracking four of his teeth right down the middle. Then, darkness overtook him as the many bruises closed his eyes shut and left him wheezing through swollen nostrils. He was on the brink of death. A few more hits and it would've all been over. John gurgled blood and was left bleeding in the moonlight, unrecognizable; a glistening red mess, like something fresh out of a butcher's shop.